A Surprise

Based on the television series created by Craig Bartlett

Grosset & Dunlap
An Imprint of Penguin Group (USA) Inc.

™ and © 2011 The Jim Henson Company. JIM HENSON'S mark & logo, DINOSAUR TRAIN mark & logo, characters and elements are trademarks of The Jim Henson Company. All Rights Reserved.
Published by Grosset & Dunlap, a division of Penguin Young Readers Group, 345 Hudson Street, New York, New York 10014.
GROSSET & DUNLAP is a trademark of Penguin Group (USA) Inc. Printed in the U.S.A.

The PBS KIDS logo is a registered mark of the Public Broadcasting Service and is used with permission.

http://pbskids.org/dinosaurtrain

The publisher does not have any control over and does not assume any responsibility for author or third-party websites or their content.

Library of Congress Cataloging-in-Publication Data is available.

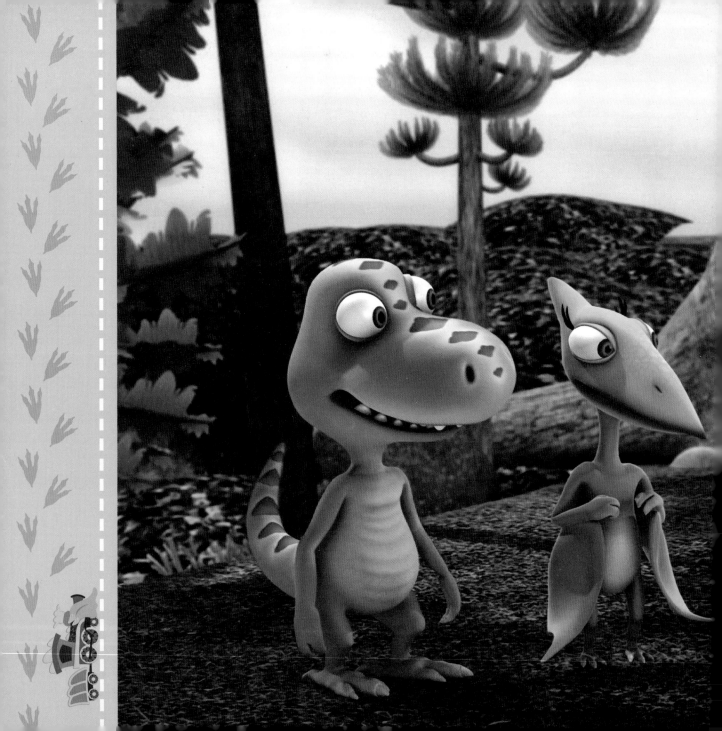

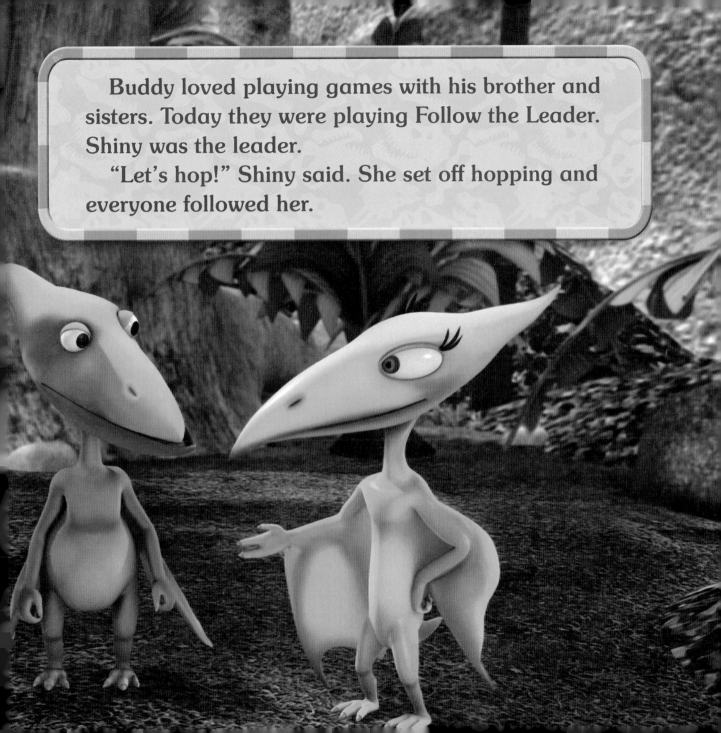

Buddy loved playing games with his brother and sisters. Today they were playing Follow the Leader. Shiny was the leader.

"Let's hop!" Shiny said. She set off hopping and everyone followed her.

"This is fun! I love hopping!" Don said.
Don closed his eyes and kept jumping.
Hop, hop, hop.
Don hopped right past Shiny!

Shiny opened her eyes and saw Don in front of her.
"Don, we're done hopping. We're twirling now," she said.

Buddy and Shiny began to twirl.
"Buddy, watch out!" Tiny shouted as
Buddy twirled closer to the nest. "You almost
stepped on Mom's flowers!"

"That reminds me. You wanted to look
for flowers for Mom today," Buddy said
to Tiny.

"Yeah! Today is Mom's special day," said
Tiny. "We're giving her the day off!"
    "Ooh, a day just for Mom," said Don.
"Let's get her a special present!"

Just then, Mrs. Pteranodon flew back to the nest. "Guess what, Mom!" said Tiny. "Dad's taking us to the Big Pond. You get the day off!"

"A day off!" squawked Mrs. Pteranodon. "That sounds so relaxing. I'm going to take a nap on the warm rocks. Have fun, kids!"

Mr. Pteranodon took the kids and flew off to the Dinosaur Train.

"Greetings, Pteranodon family. Where are you off to today?" asked Mr. Conductor.

Don and Shiny held up their tickets.
"We're going to the Big Pond," said Shiny.
"We're going to find a special present for
our mom," said Tiny.

Mr. Pteranodon and the kids got off the train and walked up to the Big Pond.

"Look, Buddy," said Tiny. "Flowers. I bet Mom would like some big red ones!"

"Ooh, shiny shells," said Shiny. "I'll make Mom a crown of the shiniest shells I can find. And one for me, too!"

Don flew up to a ledge. "I'm going to catch the *biggest* fish in this pond!"

"Look, Dad. A big splash," said Don.
"You know what that means," said Mr.
Pteranodon. "A big fish!"

Don and Mr. Pteranodon dove into the water to catch the big fish. But all they caught was a very small fish!

Suddenly Mr. Pteranodon heard a squawk.
He looked up and saw Don carrying a *huge*
fish. "Way to go, Don!" he shouted.

Meanwhile, Shiny began separating her shells. "One pile for shiny shells, one pile for *shinier* shells, and one pile for *super* shiny shells," she said.

Just then Shiny spotted a new shell. "You are super-*super* shiny," she said. Shiny looked around. "Yep, I need a new pile!"

In the woods, Buddy and Tiny saw a bee. "Buddy," said Tiny, "bees *love* flowers. Let's follow him!" The bee flew off into a patch of pink flowers.

"These are nice," said Buddy, "but not quite right. Come on, bee, help us find some big red flowers for Mom!"

Buddy and Tiny chased after the bee. It led them right to a field of big red flowers! "These are perfect," said Tiny as they chose some. "Let's go show everyone else!"

Buddy and Tiny raced back to the Big
Pond. Everyone was waiting for them.
"Come on, Team Pteranodon," said
Mr. Pteranodon. "Let's get these presents
back to the Dinosaur Train!"

That night, back at the nest, the kids gave Mrs. Pteranodon her gifts.

"I made you a crown of the shiniest shells," said Shiny.

"I got you a big fish!" said Don.

"And we found some big red flowers for your garden!" shouted Buddy and Tiny.

"Wow! These are such thoughtful gifts," said
Mrs. Pteranodon. "I'm the luckiest mom in the
world!"